Little Owl's Night

by Divya Srinivasan

VIKING

An Imprint of Penguin Group (USA) Inc.

Little Owl's Night

by Divya Srinivasan

VIKING

An Imprint of Penguin Group (USA) Inc.

Little Owl was having a wonderful night.

He watched the funny possum family waddle along in a neat row.

Hedgehog sniffed around the mushroom patch.

Skunk was eating berries because he could find no snails.

By the river, beavers gnawed at trees.

Turtle hid in her shell as fireflies danced all around.

Little Owl visited his friend the raccoon.
As they sat in the clover, fog rolled in and
hovered just overhead.

Moths fluttered toward the moon.
Silver dust fell from their wings.

Little Owl wanted to follow, but it was time to head home.

On the way, Little Owl flew by Grumbly Cave.
Bear was inside, snoring up a storm.

"Wake up, Bear! Don't sleep all night!"
Little Owl sang. "I want to show you the moon!"

But the bear kept snoring, as usual.
Little Owl flew home to his tree, gazing at the sky.

He wondered if the bear had ever seen stars.

Little Owl sat on his branch.
How he loved the night forest!

Frog croaked softly.

Cricket chirped smartly.

Little Owl heard rustling at the foot of his tree. Fox had come to say hello.

It was late now. The bats were gliding home.
"Mama," Little Owl whispered, "tell me again
how night ends."

"The moon and stars fade to ghosts," Mama said.
"Spiderwebs turn to silver threads.
Dewdrops sparkle on leaves and grass like tiny
stars come down.

Moonflowers close and morning glories open.

The sky brightens from black to blue,

blue to red,

red to gold.

"The rooster crows. The crows caw.
And the day begins," said Mama.

But Little Owl did not hear.

He was fast asleep.

For Amma, Appa, and Ramya.
I'm so lucky to have you.
—Divya

VIKING
Published by Penguin Group
Penguin Young Readers Group, 345 Hudson Street, New York, New York 10014, U.S.A.
Penguin Group (Canada), 90 Eglinton Avenue East, Suite 700, Toronto, Ontario, Canada M4P 2Y3
(a division of Pearson Penguin Canada Inc.)
Penguin Books Ltd, 80 Strand, London WC2R 0RL, England
Penguin Ireland, 25 St Stephen's Green, Dublin 2, Ireland (a division of Penguin Books Ltd)
Penguin Group (Australia), 250 Camberwell Road, Camberwell, Victoria 3124, Australia
(a division of Pearson Australia Group Pty Ltd)
Penguin Books India Pvt Ltd, 11 Community Centre, Panchsheel Park, New Delhi – 110 017, India
Penguin Group (NZ), 67 Apollo Drive, Rosedale, Auckland 0632, New Zealand
(a division of Pearson New Zealand Ltd.)
Penguin Books (South Africa) (Pty) Ltd, 24 Sturdee Avenue, Rosebank, Johannesburg 2196, South Africa

Penguin Books Ltd, Registered Offices: 80 Strand, London WC2R 0RL, England

First published in 2011 by Viking, a division of Penguin Young Readers Group

5 7 9 10 8 6 4

Copyright © Divya Srinivasan, 2011
All rights reserved

LIBRARY OF CONGRESS CATALOGING-IN-PUBLICATION DATA

Srinivasan, Divya.
Little Owl's night / by Divya Srinivasan.
p. cm.
Summary: Little Owl enjoys a lovely night in the forest visiting his friend the raccoon,
listening to the frogs croak and the crickets chirp, and watching the fog that hovers overhead.
ISBN 978-0-670-01295-4 (hardcover)
Special Markets ISBN 978-0-670-78484-4 Not for resale
[1. Owls—Fiction. 2. Night—Fiction. 3. Forests and forestry—Fiction.
4. Forest animals—Fiction.] I. Title.
PZ7.S77414Li 2011   [E]—dc22   2010049513

Manufactured in China   Set in Gararond

This Imagination Library edition is published by Penguin Young Readers, a division
of Penguin Random House, exclusively for Dolly Parton's Imagination Library,
a not-for-profit program designed to inspire a love of reading and learning, sponsored
in part by The Dollywood Foundation. Penguin's trade editions of this work are
available wherever books are sold.